Dance

With Me,

Baby

A Yeah, Baby Novella

FIONA DAVENPORT

Copyright

Love is a lot like
dancing—you just
surrender to
the music.

~Unknown~

Prologue

Declan

I've never really cared about ballet. That's not to say I didn't like it, I simply hadn't thought about it. As a doctor, I didn't have a lot of time for new hobbies and interests. But, when your best friend's incredibly pregnant wife has tickets to see New York City Ballet perform *La Bayadère* and she starts crying when you politely decline... That's how I ended up spending my first night off in over a month watching flying tutus and men in tights.

There really were no bad seats in the theatre, but sitting in left center orchestra was how the ballet became the center of my world. Or, more accurately, one specific ballet dancer. She was dancing on my side of the stage, her pink costume hugging her long, lithe body in all of the right places. Under the bright lights, her skin looked lustrous and her brown hair shimmered in its slicked back bun.

I was completely captivated and she became the star of the performance. At one point, her eyes swept over our section and my breath caught in my throat as I viewed gorgeous violet eyes. For a brief moment, our gazes collided and I swore the world stopped turning.

My body came to life for the first time in, I didn't even know how long. My heart was racing, my skin tingling, and my trousers were uncomfortably tight for the rest of the show, but I barely noticed.

When the last song was played and the dancers had retreated from the stage, I couldn't tear my eyes away. I was hoping for even just the tiniest glimpse of my ballerina.

"Declan."

I was hurtled back into the real world by the sound of Nancy's voice and her hand on my shoulder. She and Kevin were standing in the row, looking at me curiously.

"Are you ready to go?" she asked. I nodded and stood, hoping the dim lighting hid the heat on my face. We exited into the aisle and Nancy slipped her arm through mine, looking up at me excitedly. "I have a surprise for you!"

Kevin groaned. "Nancy, you didn't." He glared at where her hands grasped my arm and quickly pulled her away, tucking her into his side.

She looked at him with wide, innocent eyes. "What?" He just shook his head, and she shrugged before turning back to me. "My friend Lisa just joined NYCB and tonight was her first performance with them."

I narrowed my eyes at Nancy but tried to keep the dark scowl off of my face. I reserved it for Kevin instead.

He put up his arms up in surrender. "Dude, I had nothing to do with this."

Nancy huffed, ignoring him and chattering on about her friend. I pretended to listen while my mind wandered back to my ballerina.

"She invited us to get together with some of the cast—"

That got my attention. "Wait, what?"

"We're"—she jerked her thumb at Kevin—"going to a cast party if you want to come. I really think you'd like Lisa. Please?"

Even if I could have resisted her begging, watery eyes, it wasn't necessary. What if my girl was there? This was my chance to find her. "Sure, why not?" Nancy squealed excitedly, and I decided not to burst her little bubble by telling her I had no intention of getting to know her friend.

Somebody had booked a large industrial loft in Soho and there had to be at least two hundred people milling around. At six foot four, I stood at least a head taller than most of the room's occupants and I continually swept the crowd in search of a pair of stunning violet eyes.

Nancy had the opposite problem and couldn't see much from her perch at barely over five feet. "Stay right here," she told me, patting my arm. "I'll go find my friend." Kevin grabbed her hand before she could get lost in the throngs of people.

"This is your chance, Dec. Make a run for it," he murmured loud enough from my ears only. I took his advice and started wading through the crowd in the opposite direction. An hour later, I was incredibly frustrated and starting to lose hope. I paused by a large, floor-to-ceiling window and scanned the crowd again.

I shifted and something dug into my back prompting me to look down at the source of my discomfort. It wasn't a window; it was a door. Pushing down the handle, I stepped out into the night, the crisp fall air blowing across a rooftop terrace. I let the door swing closed behind me and walked over to a tall, metal railing. The view of the city was incredible, but it was nothing compared to what I saw when I glanced to my left.

A small group of people in a cozy seating area, huddled around an outdoor heater, chatting and laughing. My eyes were completely fixated on a brunette with high cheekbones, almond shaped eyes, and a cupid's bow mouth.

She threw her head back and laughed, and I wanted to trace the graceful lines of her neck with my tongue. Her fuzzy blue sweater was formfitting and, per position, thrust her chest forward. Like many professional dancers, her tits were not large, but fuck, they were spectacular.

As though pulled by an invisible line, I began to approach the group, my eyes trained solely on my ballerina. The rest of the group, the terrace, everything, it all faded away. At about five feet away, her head lifted and rotated in my direction. Just like before, our gazes locked, but this time, she didn't have the performance to tear her away.

I closed the rest of the gap and stood next to her chair, looming over her. That's when I noticed the silence, and I broke our connection to see several pairs of eyes studying me.

"Do you mind if I borrow this beautiful lady?" I asked lightly, making sure there was pleasant humor in my tone. I didn't want to scare her off by betraying how desperately I wanted to simply toss her over my shoulder and run away to some place where I could keep her all to myself.

More silence. I held my hand out to my violet-eyed girl and waited. I hoped somewhere inside her, she understood that if she accepted this gesture, she would no longer have a choice. She would be mine.

It was the longest seconds of my life, but then she placed her hand in mine and sealed her fate. I helped her to stand and then placed my hand on the small of her back and led her away to a dark, empty corner of the roof.

When we were hidden from the view of others, I ran out of patience and slowly lowered my mouth to hers. At first, it was a few light brushes, but it wasn't enough, so I licked along her bottom lip, requesting entrance. She parted them immediately, earning a growl of approval from deep in my chest. My hands had found their way to her lower back, and I clenched the fabric in my fists as I pulled her body flush against mine.

She tasted amazing, and the sound of a soft moan took my annoying erection straight to a fucking baseball bat. Damn, I wanted her. I needed privacy, a bed, and our naked skin touching.

I finally lifted my head and smiled at the dazed expression on her face. "What is your name, my beautiful ballerina?"

"Juliette," she whispered. "Juliette Moureaux."

Even her name was sexy. I ran a finger across her cupid's bow. "Juliette," I repeated, loving the way her name rolled off of my tongue. "I'm Declan McGowan."

I kissed her again, unable to stop myself, and when I was on the very brink of losing it and fucking her against the wall, I tore my lips away. Looking deeply into her eyes, I decided to take a leap. Going slow wasn't my style. When I wanted something, I went after it, full speed ahead. She might as well learn that about me from the get-go.

"Come home with me," I demanded, careful to keep my voice gentle but firm.

She pursed her lips, which was insanely adorable, and only made my desire for her grow. Her expression tinged with worry, and I knew I wasn't going to be happy about whatever she said next.

"I've never done something like that. I'm so tempted, Declan, you have no idea, but—"

"Good," I interrupted her, not the least interested in what she had to say after "but." I started to guide her back inside until she stopped and tugged my suit coat to keep me from continuing.

"But, I'm not sure it's a good idea. I'm leaving tomorrow for a four month, international tour."

Her words hit me like a ton of bricks. *Tomorrow?* I grabbed her hand and held it tight, I couldn't let her go. *Could I?* No, I had to convince her to stay. "All the more reason for us to make the most of this night." I almost choked on the words.

"The thing is . . . there's something about you, Declan. I just know you're someone I could fall really hard for."

That was it, I was done with the conversation. I lifted her against my chest and went inside, threading my way through the crowd until I reached the nearest exit. To my surprise, she wound her arms around my neck and laid her head on my chest, not uttering another word of protest. When I reached the sidewalk, I told her to hold on and raised my hand from her back to hail a cab.

Setting her inside, I followed when she scooted across the bench seat. "42nd and 5th," I told the driver before hauling Juliette onto my lap and slanting my mouth over hers. Typical New York cabbie, he raced through the streets like a bat out of hell, hitting the brakes hard as we reached my apartment building.

I swiped my card and didn't let go of Juliette as I got out of the car. After kicking the door shut, I stalked into my building, nodding at the doorman who opened my private elevator so I could march straight in. The door closed and I crashed my mouth down over hers. I dropped Juliette's feet to the ground, then bent my knees so I could grip the globes of her incredible ass and lift her, forcing her legs around my waist.

Moving forward, I pressed her back to the wall and ground my cock into the heat between her thighs. She cried out and it took every fucking ounce of my strength not to come right then and there. I was saved by the ding of the elevator letting me know we'd reached the penthouse on the fourteenth floor. It opened up right into my living room and I headed straight for the couch, unable to make it any farther.

I lowered us both down onto the cushions, my mouth releasing hers so we could both catch our breath. My hands tunneled under her sweater, shoving it up over her head and off. Then I popped the catch of her bra and my mouth instantly watered. Her tits were fucking perfect. Round and creamy, tipped with hard, pink little peaks. I swooped down and took one in my mouth, nibbling and sucking while she moaned and shivered beneath me.

My control was wearing thin and I wanted to taste her pussy before I took her, so I slid down her body. She was wearing black sailor pants, buttoned over her flat belly. Amazingly, I didn't rip off any of the brass discs in my haste to remove her bottoms. The same cannot be said of the virginal, lacy white panties I found underneath. I dropped my head to bury my nose against her, inhaling deeply, filling my lungs with the scent of her arousal.

The fabric was soaked clear through and it ripped away easily when I tugged at the seams. Without any more barriers, I used two fingers to open her lips wide and lick up the center. I groaned at the burst of flavor on my tongue. She tasted even better than she smelled.

"This pussy," I moaned. "Damn, Juliette. I want to fucking live between your legs. You're so wet, I could drink from you and never go thirsty."

Her body was taut, vibrating with tension, and my words caused her hips to buck up sharply. I started licking and sucking, plunging my tongue inside her, doing everything but letting her break until she was screaming my name, her hands threaded in my hair, holding my face to her pussy.

When I felt like she couldn't take any more, I stiffened my tongue and drove it insider her as I pinched her clit, and she screamed as she shuddered violently, her orgasm ripping through her. I kept thrusting inside her and tugging at her clit until she crested again, then I leisurely licked her as she floated back down to earth.

My cock was ready to bust through my dress pants and I quickly shucked them, along with my suit coat and shirt. I started to settle over her, my cock almost touching her heat when she grabbed my biceps and held me at a distance. *What the fuck?*

"Condom," she panted. I opened my mouth to argue, I didn't want anything between us, ever. In fact, I was shocked at how anxious I felt to put my baby inside her belly. However, until we had a chance to really talk, it was probably a good idea. I lifted her into my arms and rushed to the bedroom. After laying her down on the bed, I flew into the bathroom and searched. And searched. *Fuck!* I hadn't been with a woman since I moved to New York City almost two years ago. I wasn't sure if I even had any.

The whole time I was searching, I was arguing with myself about whether to simply forget about it and eat her until she did too. But, I finally came across an old package buried in a travel bag under the sink.

When I stepped out of the bathroom, I growled in complete approval of the sight in front of me. Juliette was sprawled out, spread eagle on the bed, her violet eyes glowing as they perused my body from head to toe. Her gaze lingered on my cock, and I could see her anxiety over my large size.

I gripped the base as I walked slowly towards her, pumping the length a couple of times. "Relax, baby. I promise, I'll fit inside your tight pussy just perfectly." I reached her side and held her face in my palms. "Trust me to make it good for you, okay?" She melted and nodded with a smile. I rolled one of the condoms down my shaft, then kissed her as I climbed onto the bed and came down on top of her.

As our skin touched, I was again fighting the need to spill my seed before I even got inside her. A few deep breaths and I was able to calm down. I spread her legs wide and lined up my cock with her pussy. Slowly, inch by inch, I pushed inside, stopping to let her adjust after each progression. Until I hit something and couldn't go any further.

I speared up onto my elbows and stared down at her. "Juliette? Baby, are you a virgin?" I asked with awe.

She nodded and blushed deeply, which was just as sexy as everything else about her.

My face split in a grin so big it almost hurt my face. She was already mine, but it felt fucking mind-blowing to know she would only ever be mine. There was no one before me and there would be no one after.

In that moment, I fought every instinct to pull out and rip off the condom before thrusting back in and taking her naturally, the way it should always be between us. But, I kept my focus on the few obstacles we would face come morning and held onto my convictions.

"Look at me, Juliette," I commanded, then waited until she complied. "Keep your eyes on mine, okay? It's going to hurt for just a second." She'd barely agreed before I thrust in all the way, burying my cock in her pussy. She cried out and her eyes filled with tears, but she kept them locked with mine. When I saw the fog of pain start to dissipate, I shifted to see if she was ready. She mewled in pleasure, and I began to lazily drive in and out, slowly picking up the tempo, using her cries and moans as a gauge.

My girl was wild and she writhed and screamed in ecstasy when I was driving in so hard the headboard banged into the wall. "You feel unbelievable, Jules. Your pussy is so tight, squeezing me so hard. Oh, fuck yes!"

Her legs gripped my waist, and I braced my feet on the footboard to give me added leverage before sliding my hands up to her tits. I pinched and plucked at her nipples, occasionally biting.

"Yes! Oh, Declan, yes! Yes!" she shouted over and over.

I moved a hand down to slip under her thigh and prop the leg over my shoulder, deepening the angle, then put pressure on her clit, causing her to scream the fucking roof down as she fell apart in my arms. Her walls closed around my cock and I couldn't hold it any longer.

"Juliette! Oh, fuck! Fuck! That's it baby! Fuuuuuck!" I bellowed as I came so hard I almost blacked out.

That was only the first time, we fucked like rabbits through the rest of the night. But, in between, we got to know each other a little bit. She talked about her dreams for her career, and I told her about how I'd ended up in New York, head of Pediatric surgery. I'd fulfilled most of my professional goals, but Juliette was on the cusp of achieving hers. By morning, one thing was clear to me. It would be the hardest fucking thing I would ever do in my whole damn life. I had to let her go.

But, make no mistake, this was temporary. One day, I would come for her and she'd better be damn well prepared because this was the last time I would ever watch her walk away from me.

Chapter 1

Juliette
Four Months Later

"You're pregnant."

I was certain I'd misunderstood my doctor's announcement. "I'm sorry, can you repeat that for me please?"

"You're pregnant." Nope, the words didn't change the second time around like I'd expected them to do. Sure, I'd been feeling a little off and had gained some weight, but not for one minute did I ever think the reason was because I was carrying a baby. "Since your cycle is irregular, I'll want to schedule an ultrasound to better pinpoint your due date. Normally we'd estimate it using the last period, but that isn't possible with the sporadic nature of yours."

I shook my head because there wasn't any need for an ultrasound to determine how far along I was. If I was pregnant, I knew exactly when it had happened. There was only one possibility, I just didn't know *how* it happened. But she misunderstood and explained further. "It's nothing to be worried about. Amenorrhea, or the cessation of periods, isn't unusual in female athletes. The intensity of your training and diet as a ballerina can negatively impact your hormonal balance."

I held my hand up to stop the flow of information. "I've been dancing all my life. The abnormality of my cycle isn't anything new to me, but the pregnancy is."

"Ahhh, yes, sorry." The doctor blushed and mumbled an apology. "I do tend to prattle on sometimes."

"And apparently I tend to get a little snippy when I'm pregnant. Sorry about that, but this news has come as a complete surprise to me. I thought the stress of my first international tour was to blame for my irritability and weight gain."

"I'd hardly call four pounds a weight gain," she teased.

"Yeah, well, tell that to my dancing partner," I muttered. "He complained about each additional pound during our lifts and suggested I lay off the pasta when we were in Italy."

"I'm afraid to say it, but my instructions are bound to make him complain even further since I'd like to see you gain at least twenty-five pounds during the course of your pregnancy," she advised gently. "And you're going to need to modify your dancing to accommodate your growing belly. During the first trimester, you may feel like you can do almost anything, but there will be changes you're going to need to make. I'm not saying you can't dance at all, Juliette, but it's vital for you to listen to your body throughout your pregnancy so you don't push yourself too far."

It was a good thing I was sitting down or else my knees might have given out as I considered the ramifications of the news she'd given me. I lifted my shift to expose my stomach and was shocked to see a tiny baby bump. *How had I missed this?* "I'm already four months along," I admitted softly.

She glanced down at the laptop she'd brought in and hit a few buttons. "That's certainly a possibility with the date of your last period, but there's no way to know for sure considering their irregularity."

"Trust me, I know beyond a shadow of a doubt that I got pregnant four months ago." She raised her eyebrows and looked at me questioningly. "It's when I lost my virginity."

"Ohhh," she drawled as understanding hit. "And no sexual activity since then?"

"Only in my dreams since he was here while I was touring Europe." Those dreams were no joke, either. He'd come to me each and every night I was gone, tormenting me with my need for him. I relived all the things he'd done to my body during the night I'd spent with him. Over and over again. Waking up with your hand in your panties and your heart thundering when you were sharing a room with another ballerina was not my idea of fun. I was just lucky she was a deep sleeper and hadn't caught me in an embarrassing position.

"It seems we have a different reason to schedule your ultrasound then, since we're nearing the usual time for a mid-pregnancy scan." I got a lump in my throat at hearing the term 'mid-pregnancy.' I felt like I'd missed out on so much of it already. "Although the main purpose of the scan is to check that your baby is developing normally, we may also be able to tell if you're expecting a boy or girl. You may want to bring the baby's father, a family member, or a friend with you since it's such a special moment."

The baby's father. I had to be the only woman ever who lost her virginity during a one-night stand, got knocked up, even though they used condoms every single time that night, and didn't realize she was pregnant for four months! Oh my goodness, this meant I had to face Declan again. *How mortifying.*

I didn't have any other choice, though. There was no getting around it since I needed to tell him I was pregnant. I didn't even have his phone number, which meant my only choice was to drop in on him unannounced at his apartment. He was bound to think I was either lying to him or that I'd kept the pregnancy a secret for the past few months.

The rest of what the doctor had to say went in one ear and out the other as I agonized over what to tell Declan and when. As I stumbled out of the office with all sorts of paperwork in my hand, I glanced at my watch and heaved a huge sigh of relief at what time it was. My visit to Declan would have to wait since my ballet mistress had organized a welcome home party for those of us who'd been on tour together.

The last thing I wanted to do was attend a party of any kind, not after having this bombshell dropped on me, but I didn't want to let her down. Plus, it sure didn't hurt that I had the perfect excuse to wait until tomorrow to face Declan. And with my stomach growling, I was reminded of my need to eat for two.

I hurried along the street, choosing to walk the six blocks between the doctor's office and the restaurant instead of catching a cab. The fresh air helped me to clear my head and focus on what was important. As I walked into the restaurant, I was still scared about all the changes the baby would bring, but I was also tremendously excited. There was a tiny life growing inside me, one Declan and I had created together. I might not have any idea what to do next yet, but I refused to regret this baby. Not even for a moment.

"Europe must have agreed with you, darling," Serena murmured as she air kissed me on both sides of my cheeks. As the company's ballet mistress, her job was to give the daily classes for the dancers and to rehearse the ballets in the company repertoire. She was a harsh task master, but I'd always had a good relationship with her. "You're practically glowing."

I was sorely tempted to blurt out my news to her right then and there. It was a conversation which was going to happen soon anyway, but we were interrupted by one of the dancers who'd joined the company when I was getting ready to leave for my tour.

"Juliette, this is Lisa Morisette, a newer member of the corps."

"It's a pleasure to meet you."

"I'm sorry to interrupt you," Lisa offered. "I wanted to tell you how excited I am to dance with you. I didn't get a chance to tell you how amazing you were as Gamzatti in *La Bayadère.* I looked for you at the cast party the night before you left but never managed to find you."

"Yes, I left a little early." I left the 'so I could go get knocked up by the sexiest man ever' unsaid, figuring I shouldn't blurt it out to a virtual stranger.

"Well at least I got the chance to meet you tonight before I got distracted by my blind date."

"Blind date?"

"Yeah, one of my friends has been telling me about her husband's best friend ever since I moved here. From everything she's said, he sounds too good to be true. Handsome, smart, kind," she rattled off.

"Mmmhmm," I murmured non-committally, trying to think of a way to get out of this conversation gracefully. She seemed like a sweet girl, but I wasn't really in the mood to discuss someone else's dating life considering the state of mine.

"Oh, wow," Lisa sighed dreamily, her attention suddenly riveted towards the door. "Nancy was not exaggerating when she described him. We were supposed to meet up a while back, but it fell through. It took her forever to get him to agree again, but damn was he worth the wait. Talk about tall, dark, and handsome."

My head swiveled to the side and my gaze landed on the man she was so delighted to meet. He was easy to spot since his tall, muscular frame towered over everyone else. A lock of his thick, dark hair had fallen onto his forehead, and my fingers itched to sweep it to the side. His fierce brown eyes were scanning the room like he owned it, while his firm lips were stretched into a taut line. There was no denying he was worth waiting for, especially not when you considered that I'd spent the last four months unable to get the thought of him out of my head. Or my heart.

Lisa's blind date was none other than Declan McGowan—the father of my unborn child. And it seemed Lisa and I weren't the only ones excited to see him because the baby chose that exact moment, while my head was already spinning, to kick for the very first time. I didn't know whether to laugh, cry, or faint.

Chapter 2

Declan

I felt a little bit of déjà vu as my eyes swept a room full of dancers once again. I'd kept my night with Juliette to myself, not ready to share her with anyone else yet. Unfortunately, it led to my best friend's matchmaking wife harassing me constantly about meeting her friend. It probably made me a complete asshole, but when her last attempt to nag me included the information that the event was a party for the returning dancers, I finally agreed to 'attend' it. I made it clear I was not going on a blind date though. It looked like she'd ignored me, because she and Kevin were nowhere to be found.

I'd waited four months, as patiently as I could, but I was done. Living without Juliette any longer was not an option, and it was time she knew it too. My eyes landed on a pretty, blonde woman, working her way towards me through the crowd, an eager look on her face. *Shit.* Nancy clearly hadn't told her friend about my adamant refusal for a date. I needed to figure out how to handle this without being a complete douche. All considerations on that front went flying out the window when I spotted the woman she'd been talking to.

I would recognize those beautiful violet pools anywhere, but she was different. She'd filled out a little bit, her skin was practically glowing, and her eyes . . . were filled with tears. She turned and headed in the opposite direction and before I could take a step forward, I was faced with the evidence of Nancy's meddling.

"Declan?" she asked, her eyes bright and a wide smile on her face. I tried not to scowl at her interference.

"You must be Lisa. It's nice to meet you. Listen, I'm sorry Nancy gave you the wrong impression, but I'm actually seeing someone, so it would be ungentlemanly of me to lead you on in any way," I rambled.

Her face fell and I felt like a jerk. *I'm going to kick your ass, Kevin*. But, I didn't have time to dwell on it, Juliette was fast disappearing. "I really am very sorry, Lisa, but you'll have to excuse me." I stepped around her and started after my woman. She turned a corner and I plowed through the crowd, determined to get to her.

I found myself in a darkened hallway and exploring a little farther in, I discovered the doors for the restrooms. Two women were just exiting and both stopped whispering as they walked by me. I ignored them and slammed through the door they'd just exited. Juliette was standing at the counter, her hands under the faucet, her eyes shocked and wide as she stared at me. A woman at the other end was in much the same position, and I glared at her. "Out."

She frowned at me, but she must have seen the murderous look in my eyes, because she grabbed a stack of paper towels, along with her purse, and scurried out of the room. Once she was gone, and it was clear the other stalls were empty, I flipped the lock on the door and stalked towards my sweet Juliette.

The room was plush and fancy, gold wall paper and fixtures, red carpet, and the thing I was most interested in, a red, velvet couch. I casually walked over and took a seat. "Juliette," I greeted.

She patted her face with water, then dried it and her hands before turning to face me. "Declan, how nice to see you." Her words were stiff and she wouldn't look me in the eyes. "You're being awfully rude to your date; don't you think?" She finally looked at me and I was temporarily lost in the turbulent purple orbs.

I raised a single eyebrow. "Date?"

She huffed, "Yes, your blind date with one of the other dancers. Holing up in the women's powder room seems quite the poor date etiquette."

I grinned when I realized what her attitude was all about. "You're so cute when you're jealous, Jules."

Her jaw dropped in surprise, but her cheeks tinged with pink. I stood and prowled over to her, cupping her face and brushing my lips along hers. "You look fucking incredible, Juliette. How did you get more beautiful?"

Her face flamed, the pink deepening to a red flush over her upper body. The off the shoulder, silky peasant blouse she was wearing showed off a great deal of skin, and I was mesmerized by the color stealing over it. My eyes dropped to her cleavage, and I growled at the low cut of her top. But that was an argument for another time.

"Why were you running from me, baby?" I asked softly.

She shook her head and her shoulder jumped in a little shrug. "I didn't want to interrupt your date and I didn't know if"—

she paused and looked everywhere but at me, until I forced her face back to mine, so close our gazes where locked—"if you'd be happy to see me again. I mean, we were a one-night stand and—"

I cut her off with my mouth crashing down over hers. I took advantage of her stunned state and pushed my tongue into her mouth. A ragged groan reverberated from deep in my chest. I felt as though those four months had been an eternity, and though I'd never doubted my decision, it was still a confirmation that she was made for me. That I couldn't live without her.

"Of course I'm happy to see you. And, I'm not on a date, so I don't have to feel guilty for this." I kissed her again and my hands found their way to her ass, lifting her so her legs wrapped around my waist, then stumbling back to drop onto the couch. She straddled my lap and her skirt bunched around her upper thighs. All that separated us was my pants and the thin layer of her panties.

"You taste every bit as amazing as I remember," I mumbled against her lips. "I bet you're just as wet for me too." I slid my hands up her sides and she tensed for a moment, but relaxed when I cupped her tits. I pulled back and looked down at the globes, something was different. Using my index fingers, I tugged down her top and stared. Juliette's modest breasts were a delicious mouthful, but small enough that she could easily go braless. So, I was taken aback to see them spilling out of the lacy cups.

"I'm not seeing things, right?" I queried absently. "Your tits are bigger." She froze, and I worried that she thought I had a problem with it. "Not that I'm complaining," I hurried to assure her. "You've filled out a little and it's sexy as fuck, baby."

"You—um—you're not so bad yourself," she said, her pink blush returning.

"I love the way you blush, Jules. It's like pouring strawberry syrup over my favorite dessert. All I want to do is eat you."

She moaned and my already hard cock grew, threatening to rip through my pants to reach her heated pussy. I could already feel the pre-come leaking from the manly instinct to breed my woman.

I reached around her to unhook her bra, but she pushed my hands away, making me growl in frustration. Four months. Four fucking months I had waited for her and my ability to go slow was slim to none.

"I think we should talk before this goes any further."

"After." My mouth chased hers, seeking a taste, but she played a mean game of keep away. I sighed and sat back. "What would you like to talk about?"

She cleared her throat and squirmed a little, rubbing her pussy over my erection. I grabbed her hips to keep her from moving any more. If she wanted any chance to keep my attention while she 'talked,' I needed her to remain still.

"Go ahead, baby. I'm listening," I murmured. Leaning in, I placed my lips on her collarbone, nibbling, licking, and leaving little bites all over her neck.

"Well, I found out—um—that's very distracting, Declan. This is important."

"So is this, Jules." I kissed my way down her cleavage while she sputtered for a response. Tugging down her bra, I kissed each rosy nipple, encouraged to take one in my mouth when she moaned again.

My hands drifted down, intent on touching her everywhere. They landed on her stomach and it was my turn to freeze. I felt all around the area, finding it odd she would gain weight in such a concentrated area. Except, I knew that wasn't what I was feeling. Pride and an abundance of love burst through me, hoping I was right.

I glanced up and she had her hands over her mouth, her eyes filled with frightened tears. Was she not happy about this? I gripped the hem of her shirt and pulled it off over her head. Then I dropped my eyes to her belly and sure enough, there was a little bump. The most beautiful little bump in the world.

I met her violet gaze and there was wonder in my voice when I asked, "We're having a baby?"

Chapter 3

Juliette

Was this really how Declan was going to find out I was pregnant? In the women's restroom of a restaurant while I was topless and sitting on his lap? This was even worse than I'd imagined when I pictured myself surprising him at his apartment to tell him the news.

I started to scramble off his lap, but when I glanced down, my eyes were riveted by the sight of his hands on my belly. I never thought I'd feel his hands on me again. Not during any of the months I'd been gone. Not even after I found out I was expecting his baby from our one night of passion. And certainly not when I saw him at the door and knew he was the blind date Lisa had been prattling on about— something I'd managed to forget when his lips had landed on mine.

It wasn't something I could ignore any longer, though. I jerked away from Declan, grabbing my top from the floor and pulling it back on. After a couple deep breaths, I turned around and faced him. "Yes, I'm pregnant with your baby." His eyes jumped from my belly to my face, and I could have sworn they were filled with happiness, but it had to be wishful thinking on my part. I tended to babble when I was nervous, and this was no exception. "I literally just found out, barely more than an hour ago. I swear I was going to come see you tomorrow and try to explain how this all happened. After I figured out what to say, that is. I wasn't going to keep the news from you, but I'm not sure I'm ready to talk to you about it yet. Not here. Not right now. I really wasn't prepared to see you tonight, let alone on a date with another woman."

"I already told you I wasn't on a date," he growled, uncoiling from where he sat on the red velvet couch and stalking towards me. "I'm not going to let you use a stupid misunderstanding as an excuse to avoid talking to me tonight. I've waited four long months for you to come home, and my patience has officially run out."

He waited, what?

"I'm sorry Lisa was mistaken about my reason for being here tonight. I didn't come for her. I came for you." He yanked me towards him, tilting my chin up with one long finger.

"How is that possible?" I whispered. "*I didn't even know I was going to be here until this morning.*"

"My best friend's wife is friends with Lisa. She's been trying to set us up for months. I wasn't the least bit interested in her matchmaking efforts and barely paid any attention to her, but when she mentioned the reason behind the party tonight, there wasn't anything that was going to keep me away."

"Lisa seemed to have missed that memo," I grumbled.

"She's clued in now. Before I hunted you down in here, I made it extremely clear to her that I'm already seeing someone and have no interest in dating anyone else."

"You're seeing someone?" I croaked, feeling sick to my stomach at the thought.

"Fuck, baby. Have you not heard a word I've been saying?" His hands gripped me around my waist and tugged until I was flush against his body, his hardened length pressed against my stomach. "Yes, I'm fucking seeing someone—*you*, the woman who's carrying my child."

Ah, right, the baby. I guessed it made sense that Declan would want to attempt to build a relationship with me now that he was aware I was pregnant with his baby. I only wished he'd been this keen to try for one before letting me go four months earlier. The logical side of me knew it had been a long-shot, considering I hadn't even known him a full day before I left for Europe, but my heart had yearned for him to ask if we could try the long-term thing while I'd been away. Only he hadn't, and this was the first time I'd heard the word 'relationship' from his delicious lips. Although, he had said I was the only reason he'd come to the party in the first place, so that had to be a good sign.

Seriously, I was going to drive myself crazy over him. Right about now, I really wished I'd spent a little less time focused on ballet and a little more time interacting with guys who weren't my dance partners. Straightening my spine, hoping to find the strength to resist him, at least for the moment, I tried to step away but he didn't let me go far. Strong hands gripped my waist and held me in place.

"Now that we've gotten that ridiculousness out of the way, I'd like to focus on what's truly important—you being pregnant with my baby." I dropped my head against his chest as tears filled my eyes. Stupid hormones. "I know you're probably scared, but I'll be with you every step of the way."

If he kept up with this sweetness, I was never going to be able to resist falling into his bed again. Even if he'd been an ass about the pregnancy, I still probably wouldn't have been able to hold out for long. Sniffling, I breathed in the masculine scent I'd missed while I'd been gone. Part of me wanted to kick myself for falling into his bed so easily, but I couldn't truly regret the most magical night of my life. All it took was one touch, one kiss, one smell and I wanted him. So much so that I had no idea how I'd ever be able to protect my heart when we were going to be connected for the rest of our lives because of the baby.

"Hey!" a feminine voice shouted through the door, interrupting my musings and startling me. "This is a public restroom, you know. The only one for women in this place, and some of us have to go. Like right now."

"Maybe we should take this conversation to somewhere a little more appropriate," I mumbled into his shirt.

"It's probably a good idea, since the last thing I need is to be arrested for indecent exposure from being caught in here with you," he chuckled. "The hospital would not approve and it wouldn't exactly be a story I'd want to share with our children later on."

"You look pretty decent to me," I sighed, stepping away from him and sweeping my gaze up his body.

"If you keep looking at me like that for much longer, there's no way in hell either of us will make it out of here with all of our clothes intact."

Kaboom! There went my panties. Seriously, they were drenched and of absolutely no use to me any longer—which only proved he was right, damn him. This time when I tried to step away, he let me go but took hold of my hand as he walked with me towards the door. With a flick of his other wrist, the bathroom door was unlocked and I was mortified when it flew open and revealed several gawking faces as they caught sight of Declan and me. I couldn't really blame them since there were rumors swirling around the company that I might be a nun in the making because I never date.

He ignored them all and hurried me out of the restaurant and into a waiting cab. The ride to his place was different than the last time, but also the same in a way. The chemistry between us still sizzled, and we were just as silent, but there was none of the kissing I'd enjoyed. Instead, Declan kept me cradled against his side while he stared down at his hand resting on my lower belly. It was just as sexy as the way he'd devoured my mouth when I'd last found myself in a cab with him. Then again, anything he did was bound to be sexy since he practically oozed sex appeal from his pores. I was no less susceptible to it tonight than I had been four months earlier, which might not bode well for me since it felt as though we were retracing our steps from that fateful evening as he led me into his building.

My legs trembled as I stepped into the elevator, remembering the way he'd practically taken me against the wall the last time I'd ridden it with him. He rubbed my back in a soothing gesture, but I barely felt it as I stared at the other side of the elevator and remembered how incredible it had felt to be wrapped around his muscular body with the heat of his erection between my legs.

Barely a minute or two passing before we reached the top floor where Declan's penthouse apartment was located. By the time the doors opened into his foyer, I was trembling with need, my doctor's warning about increased sexual drive during the second trimester playing over again in my head. This time around, it was me who led him straight to the couch and urged him onto the cushions. "This is all your fault, and you're damn well going to take care of it."

Chapter 4

Declan

"My fault?" I laughed. I let Juliette push me down onto the sofa and was more than happy to accommodate her when she straddled my lap.

"It's the stupid pregnancy hormones! I need you, Declan," she pleaded.

Holy shit. If this was what I had to look forward to during a pregnancy, Juliette would be finding herself knocked up for the foreseeable future. Of course, I wanted a big family anyway, and she'd mentioned the same when we talked on our night together. So, it was going to happen either way.

I wanted to do as she asked, in fact I was really liking the idea of making her beg me. My cock was more than ready to give her exactly what she wanted after the four-month wait. Jerking off was a poor substitute for sinking inside her silken heat, but it was all I had while she was gone. Waiting even one more minute was the last thing my body wanted, but it was exactly what I needed to do for our relationship—which meant I was forced to turn in my man card for what I had to do next.

She went in for a kiss, and I wrapped my fingers around her toned biceps to hold her slightly away from me. Hurt flashed across her face and I couldn't stand it, so I shifted my hands up to cup her face and kissed her, releasing a fraction of the passion still pent up inside me.

As soon as she began to try and get closer, to press her heat against the bulge in my slacks, I set her away again. Now she just looked confused, and maybe a little dazed from lust. There was a flush on her skin that was so beautiful, I was tempted to fuck her first, then talk later. Luckily, I was able to talk myself off the ledge. I didn't want anything hanging over us when I finally took her to bed. I wanted hours to worship her from head to toe, no interruptions, and no questions hanging over us.

"Baby, I promise, I will take care of you. Always. But, we need to talk first."

Her cupid's bow mouth turned down in an adorable pout, and I had to kiss it. She sighed and it sounded like a combination of exasperation and desire. Something so simple, and it did me in.

I captured her lips in a deep kiss and ran my palms up her thighs to her center. I brushed a finger across her panties and it was soaked right through. My groan was swallowed up by the tangling of our tongues.

"So wet. I'll take the edge off for you, baby. Okay?"

She moaned and her head dropped back, her eyes closing when I slipped a finger underneath the fabric. It was in the way, so I curled my finger around the center strip and ripped it, leaving her pussy bare. She gasped and arced her back. I ran my finger up her slit and brought it to my mouth, proceeding to suck it inside and lick it clean. She tasted so fucking delicious. I needed more.

With my hands on her waist, I encouraged her to get up onto her knees, then to her feet, so she was standing on the couch. It was the perfect fucking height. *Pun intended*. I tucked her long skirt into its waistband and drank in the sight of her pink, glistening sex. I licked my lips and then glanced up to see Juliette watching me with lust darkening her eyes to a deep purple.

I took her hands and placed them on either side of my head, so she was gripping the back of the couch. "Hold on tight, Juliette." Grasping the cheeks of her ass, I tugged her forward and buried my face in her pussy, inhaling and becoming almost delirious from her potent scent. My tongue plunged inside her and then ran up her center to circle her sensitive clit. "Ride me, baby," I grunted raggedly. I licked and nibbled her into a frenzy, forcing her to lock her legs as she fucked my face.

I took her to the brink and kept her there until she was wild and desperate, then drove two fingers inside her tight pussy and sucked her little nub hard into my mouth. She shouted my name as her knees buckled, and I held her up so I could work her through her orgasm.

As the shudders subsided, I helped her down from her perch and back into her previous position. She was so beautiful sitting there on my lap, her cheeks rosy from coming, her amethyst pools hazy with satisfaction. I took a moment to relish the fact that she was mine. My eyes dropped from her lips to her tummy and a wide grin split my face. We were going to be a family. There were only a few things that would make this even more perfect. Speaking of ...

"You know I'm ecstatic about our baby, right?" I asked enthusiastically.

Her pout turned into a deadpan expression, wariness suddenly clouding her violet eyes. She attempted to climb off of my lap but I held her hips firmly, keeping her in place. She nodded stiffly and didn't try to move again.

"Do you have an ultrasound scheduled?" I couldn't wait to see our little one. The four month wait for Juliette to return was excruciating, and I needed to fill my time with hope. I may have done some research. I knew all of her (yes, I think it's a girl) joints and limbs were fully formed and we might see her stretch, or suck her thumb, and we'd be able to see her facial expressions.

"Three days from today," she said, her tone emotionless.

I was suddenly struck by an awful thought. "Juliette, please tell me you weren't considering not keeping our child." We'd only spent one night together, but I felt like I knew her—my body, my heart, my soul. I knew her with every fiber of my being. And yet, I had to ask.

She recoiled and her expression turned horrified. "No!" Her hands curled protectively over her belly. "Absolutely not. Whatever happens with us, I'm keeping this baby."

I crushed my mouth over hers, happy to know I'd been right. When I finally pulled back, I felt it all washing over me once again and a million thoughts started colliding in my brain. "Cancel your other appointment and I'll get one scheduled for you with Dr. Frazier."

"But, I like Dr.—"

"She's the best OB in the state," I said, cutting off her protest. "Plus, her office is at my hospital, so it will make it easier for me to attend all of your appointments."

She nodded, though she certainly looked put out over it. "Bossy," she muttered. I mentally shrugged. She'd get used to it.

"I can't fucking believe we are having a baby," I breathed with awe.

"About that, how did you know it was yours?"

"What?" I was genuinely confused by her question.

"When you realized I was pregnant, you said 'we're having a baby,' you didn't ask if it was yours."

It had never occurred to me, not even once, that my beautiful dancer would get involved with someone else, that it was possible she hadn't felt the same strong connection between us. I frowned and glared at her sternly. "Because we both know you're mine. You have been since the moment I laid eyes on you." I was irritated when she didn't agree right away, but she distracted me with her next comment.

"I have no intention of keeping you from the baby, just so you know. You can be as involved as you want."

"I'm going to be there for everything, the Lamaze classes, the midnight snack runs, baby proofing the apartment. Although," I mused, "we can tackle that after you're moved in and we get married."

Chapter 5

Juliette

I leapt off his lap like a startled cat, practically hissing with irritation at the backhanded way he'd brought up marriage. Something so sacred should be treated with more respect than a casual comment to the woman you'd knocked up during a one-night stand—even if I was the woman in question and a part of me desperately wanted to accept his proposal. Or his assumption that we were going to get married since he hadn't actually bothered to propose.

"I can't—you just—this isn't—" I sputtered, unable to form a complete sentence.

"You can," he snapped, snaking an arm around my waist and pulling me back onto his lap.

"You will." He dropped a kiss on my lips when I tried to disagree with him.

"And none of this is up for debate." His hand rested on my stomach, giving it a little squeeze for emphasis.

"Forgive me for thinking I should have a say in decisions that impact my future." My sarcastic response earned me a little swat on my butt after he'd tilted me to the side. "Hey!" I yelped.

"I think you meant to say *our* future," he rumbled. "Didn't you, Jules?'

"Well, yeah. Kinda. Sorta," I mumbled, flustered by the rush of heat in my veins from the sting his hand left behind. "I mean, obviously our lives will be intertwined from now on because of the baby, but that doesn't mean you get to just proclaim that I'm going to move in and marry you. You can't expect me to meekly follow your dictate like some brainless sycophant."

"I never said I didn't expect you to need a little time to agree with me, baby," he chuckled. "Feel free to try and resist, as long as you keep in mind that it's futile because you're going to have my ring on your finger to go along with my baby in your belly. At least your defiance gives me an excuse to get creative when it comes to convincing you to say yes."

"Creative?" I gasped as his palm slid up my thigh to cup me intimately.

"How else am I supposed to get you to mindlessly agree with me except to make you lose all reason?" His question was a rumble of sound against my skin as he kissed my throat and worked his way around to my ear. "It only seems fair since you've driven me out of mine for months. It's a damn good thing our new fundraising campaign has decreased my surgery time because you've been hell on my concentration."

"Really?" I whispered back, surprised to hear he'd thought about me enough to mess with his focus.

"I couldn't seem to get you out of my head." He gripped my neck to pull me closer and dropped his forehead against mine. "Not that I tried too hard. It made me feel closer to you."

I melted, utterly enchanted by his admission. It was entirely unexpected and made me feel like maybe he wanted me for more than just the baby—and sex. I had no doubt he wanted me for that, not with the proof of his desire hard beneath me.

"And now that I have you back where you belong, you're going to have a hard time getting *me* out of *you*. I need you too badly." His tongue slid between my lips and caressed mine slowly. This kiss was softer than our others, more thorough, as he leisurely explored my mouth.

When he lifted his head, I was panting for breath and darn close to begging him to make me come again. Cradling me in his arms, he rose to his feet and carried me to his bedroom as though I was as light as a feather. When my back hit the mattress, I could only stare up at him helplessly. His dark eyes lit with appreciation as he looked down at me, making my nipples harden at the blatant arousal shining from his gaze.

My breath caught in my throat when he raised me up to lift my shirt over my head. With a flick of his wrist, he unsnapped my bra and slid it off my shoulders. I couldn't stop the whimper that escaped my lips when he traced my nipple with a fingertip and it peaked even further under his touch.

"I should make you beg me for it, but I want you too much to wait any more to feel your heat wrapped around me."

He wasn't trying to hide how I affected him, and his honesty made me want to give him a concession. Maybe just a tiny one.

"Please, Declan. Don't make either of us wait." It wasn't quite begging, but I figured it was close enough.

By the flare of approval in his eyes, it seemed he agreed. He eased my skirt over my hips and down my legs, his five o'clock shadow scraping against my sensitive skin as he nibbled his way back up my body.

"I dreamed about this pussy every single night," he murmured, his palm cupping me again. "When I took your virginity, I claimed it as mine."

The possessiveness in his tone sent shivers up my spine. I opened my legs wider to give him better access while I was splayed naked on the mattress beneath him. Lifting himself up, he practically tore his clothes from his body before moving back between my thighs. His cock pushed against me.

"I'm clean, it'd been almost two years for me before I saw you on that stage. I want to take you bare."

Two years? It didn't seem possible, considering Declan was an insanely hot doctor who was incredible in the sack. He must have interpreted my skeptical face for resistance because he continued to make his argument for going without a condom.

"I haven't so much as even looked at another woman since that night," he admitted. "And I've planted my baby inside you so there really isn't any need for one.

Besides which, we went through the entire box last time and I haven't replaced it."

"Fat lot of good that did."

"You'd think the head of Pediatric surgery would have thought to look at the expiration on a box of condoms before using them," he breathed into my ear, a hint of sheepishness in his tone. "But you had me so desperate to get inside you that I wasn't thinking clearly."

"Your condoms were expired?" I gasped. That solved the mystery of how I'd managed to get knocked up the night I lost my virginity. It was almost as though this baby was meant to be.

He nudged inside me about an inch and held still. "It's only a guess. The last thing I cared about when you left me was an empty box of condoms. I was too busy fighting myself from going after you and convincing you to stay," he whispered, right before shifting his hips and slowly sliding the rest of the way inside me.

My emotions spiraled out of control, damn my hormones and his silver tongue. Tears swam in my eyes as I closed them before I totally lost it.

"Juliette, don't hide from me," he demanded. I slowly raised my lids, and he rewarded me with a circle of his hips. "I never want to spend so much time away from you again. I want you and our baby in my life. In my home. *Our* home."

He withdrew from my body and plunged back in, making me gasp.

"Talk later. More moving now," I whimpered, rocking my hips back and forth.

He pulled out and rammed back in. "I'm happy those condoms didn't work. Thrilled as fuck that my baby is growing inside you."

"Please, Declan."

"Say you'll marry me."

"Need to come," I pleaded.

"Marry me," he repeated.

"Not like this," I breathed out.

"You want to say yes, I can see it in your eyes," he rasped, grinding his pelvis against me.

"I'm not getting engaged while we're having sex" I groaned, even as my body tightened in pleasure.

"This isn't just sex, baby. It's so much more."

He rocked gently back into me, and I moaned. Our night together had been amazing, but this was even better somehow. More intense with our eyes locked together while he leisurely plunged in and out of me. It didn't take long before I began to shudder underneath him.

"Marry me."

My head moved from side to side, both as an answer and as a sign of how close to the edge I was. My hands were clenched on the damp skin of his back, and my heels were digging into the taut flesh of his butt. Whatever it took to get his body as close to me as I could.

"Fine, tell me yes later but come for me now," he urged.

"Yes," I moaned on the next surge of his hips, my pussy clenching around his cock while fireworks burst behind my eyelids.

He pushed inside one last time before his body went rigid. Then he held himself deep and filled me with his come, rolling to the side and taking me with him when he was empty. I rested my head on his chest and listened to his heartbeat as it slowed back to normal, thinking about how much I'd missed him. I wasn't sure if it was the right decision because it seemed too much like trapping him with the pregnancy, but I went ahead and did it anyway because I didn't want to let him go.

"Yes," I sighed. "I'll marry you."

Chapter 6

Declan

I was fucking exhausted and loathed the idea of letting my woman go, even for a minute. But, a stronger part of me reacted to Juliette's agreement with a burst of energy and I jumped out of bed, turning to face her. "Don't move."

She rose up on her elbows and lifted an eyebrow but then shrugged and plopped back down. I grinned at her before spinning on my heel and rushing out, down the hall, and into my office. Quickly punching in the combination to my wall safe, I swung it open and snatched a tiny black, velvet box from inside. Then I shut the little door and hightailed it back to my beautiful dancer.

She looked at me curiously as I climbed back into bed and I pulled her up into a sitting position, ignoring her groans of protest. "You wore me out, Dec," she whined playfully. But, her face morphed into wide-eyed shock as I presented her with the box and opened it to reveal an antique engagement ring. The band was intricate gold filigree that wound up to the center and created a flower that held a two carat diamond in the center.

"Juliette Moureaux, will you marry me?" It was a question, but my tone of voice and look of resolve brooked no argument.

Her face lit up and a beautiful smile graced her lips as she stared inside the jewelry box. "You bought me a ring?" she breathed.

"Well, it's an heirloom. It belonged to my father's mother," I told her, assuming she would appreciate the special history. I wouldn't have given this ring to just anybody. If I'd never met Juliette and ended up proposing to another woman, I wouldn't have used it. It was meant for Juliette's finger, even if I wouldn't have known it, I would have felt it.

So, I was shocked when her light dimmed and she seemed to be forcing her smile. "It's beautiful, but I'm not sure I should be the one wearing it yet. I mean, it's obviously very special to you and who knows what's going to happen. Let's see how things go first, okay?"

My jaw hardened from frustration and I felt my elation deflate into hurt. I'd gone to my safety deposit box the day after Juliette left and brought this ring home. It had been burning a hole in my proverbial pocket since then. I'd thought she felt the same overwhelming truth as I had, that we were meant for each other.

I mentally shook off the melancholy thoughts and spoke with firm resolve, "Juliette, I can't make this any clearer. You. Are. Mine. You have been since you made the choice to take my hand. There is no if, and, or but, in this situation. We are getting married and there will be no discussion, *not ever*, of us separating."

Taking the ring from the box, I slid it onto the fourth finger of her left hand, and raised it to my lips. Then I crawled over her, forcing her to lay back, and caged her in with my arms on either side of her head. "We are a family—you, me, and our little peanut. Now, as excited as I am to have our baby in our life, we need to take advantage of the next five months, don't you think?"

I slammed my mouth down over hers, still clinging to the small burst of energy from before. After a few minutes, I slowed down and spent the next couple of hours worshipping every inch of her body.

When I at last allowed myself to taste her pussy, she was drenched and I lapped up every bit of her cream as I drove her to an intense orgasm. I slid up her body, our sweat soaked skin making the journey easy. Before the last of her aftershocks died, I pushed inside her, groaning at the exquisite feel of her bare pussy pulsing around my cock.

I didn't think I would ever get used to the feeling of being inside her without protection. It was heaven and I wanted to savor it for the rest of our lives. I moved slowly in and out, lazily making love to her, fascinated by her expressions, her cries of delight, every shudder and twitch of her body.

Every thrust into her, I released more of my love until we reached the height of ecstasy together. I would have given her everything, all of me, but the truth was, she already had it.

"Jules," I called down the hallway from my office, "what time should the movers be at your apartment tomorrow?"

She was in the kitchen making lunch and something clanged as it was dropped onto the stone floor. I sighed and sat back down in my chair, then asked the scheduler on the phone if I could call her back. Then I waited, knowing what was coming next. Sure enough, Juliette came to my door and glared at me, her fisted hands propped on her hips. She looked gorgeous with her violet eyes full of fire and my cock hardened at the sight.

After I'd made love to her, we'd talked for a little while, then fallen asleep in each other's arms. Even passed out cold, I couldn't bear to let her go. I was afraid I'd wake up and she'd be gone. It would be a futile attempt on her part, of course, because I'd chase her ass down and chain her to the fucking bed if I had to. I was determined to get her moved in and married to me as soon as possible.

"Excuse me?"

"Baby, I told you last night. You're moving in with me. Now, what time tomorrow? They'll pack up everything and transport it here." I frowned in thought, then narrowed my eyes in warning. "I don't want you lifting a single box, Juliette."

She glared right back at me. "I agree that I should move in, *eventually*. Definitely before the baby is born. But, you can't just decide it's going to be tomorrow! We have plenty of time to worry about that, then we'll tackle the wedding after the birth."

I almost laughed at her ridiculous comment, until I realized she was serious. "Juliette soon-to-be McGowan," I growled. "I am moving your sexy little ass in with me immediately. And, you will have my last name before our baby is born"—I held up my hand when I saw she was about to argue—"This is not up for debate, baby. But, I'm not completely unreasonable, I'll give you three months to plan a wedding, or I'm dragging you to the courthouse."

I opened a drawer in my desk and fished out an envelope, then tossed it to her. She caught it and opened is cautiously, her brow shooting to her hair line at the contents.

"Those arrived this morning. There is no limit on that credit card and the other is a temporary debit card to our checking account. We'll get you permanent ones after you change your last name." I ignored her sputtering and went on, "I expect to see plenty of charges for the wedding and baby."

"Declan—"

"If tomorrow isn't good, pick a day this week or I'll choose one for you, Jules," I interrupted stubbornly.

She made a frustrated sound and threw her hands in the air. "Fine! Tomorrow," she growled. And damn, it was cute as fuck. "I'll be done with work at three." Then she pivoted and stomped back to the kitchen. I waited as long as I could before I let the laughter burst from my lungs. So fucking adorable.

By the next night, she was almost completely moved in and I was able to heave a partial sigh of relief. After wearing her the fuck out that night, we were lying in bed and I was holding her with my hand resting on her belly when the baby kicked. It was amazing. I couldn't wait to meet our little peanut.

"Dr. McGowan, I hear congratulations are in order." Dr. Frazier grinned at me as she entered the examination room.

I beamed back at her. "For the baby or the engagement?" I was standing to the left of Juliette, holing her hand, so I lifted it to show off the ring.

Dr. Frazier laughed and patted my arm as she maneuvered around the equipment and stopped at Juliette's other side. "Both. Though, I wasn't actually aware of the engagement."

Holding out a hand, Dr. Frazier warmly introduced herself to Juliette. "I hear you're about four months, Ms. Moureaux?"

"Yes. We're positive about the conception date." Juliette blushed and I chuckled, earning myself a cute little frown. "You can call me Juliette," she added.

Dr. Frazier nodded with a smile. "Okay, shall we see if this little one wants to cooperate today?" She pulled up Juliette's shirt to just under her breasts, exposing her baby bump. After putting some gel on there, she started moving a transducer probe around and a swishing sound emanated from the machine. Then, there was a pulsing, a heartbeat, and my knees weakened a bit.

I stared at the screen and watched the little person inside my girl. I was filled with a million different emotions but when Juliette's hand tightened around mine, I swung my gaze to face her liquid purple eyes. Lowing my head, I kissed her lips gently, infusing the gesture with love and gratitude. She was my dream come true, and it was almost surreal at that moment to know she and the baby were mine.

"Do you want to know the gender?"

Chapter 7

Juliette

"Yes."

"No," I answered at the same time as Declan.

Dr. Frazier's gaze darted between the two of us before a startled laugh bubbled up her throat. "I guess I could only tell Dr. McGowan, but I doubt he'll be able to keep the secret from you for five days, let alone five long months. Why don't the two of you take a moment to discuss what you'd like to do? I'll step out to give you some privacy."

The minute the door closed behind her, Declan leaned over me, setting his hands on the exam table on either side of my head. His eyes practically glowed with happiness, and his smile was the biggest I'd ever seen.

"You think you're going to get me to agree, don't you?" I asked suspiciously.

He dropped a brief kiss on my lips before answering. "I hope you will, but that's not why I'm grinning like a fool. I'm just so damn happy to be able to experience the first decision we're facing as new parents together."

"We can't even agree on something as simple as learning the sex of our baby," I fretted, twisting the engagement ring around my finger. "We barely know each other and we're already living together, engaged to be married, and going to have a baby."

"I can't wait to learn everything there is to know about you, Juliette," he whispered against my lips after giving me another sweet kiss. "But I disagree about this being an easy decision. I'm a bit of a planner, which I'm sure isn't a surprise to you by now, but that's not why I want to know. This isn't about planning the nursery or buying baby clothes for me. I just feel this deep-seated need to learn as much about him or her as soon as I can. I'm already wondering if our baby will have your gorgeous violet eyes, if he or she will be as graceful as you, if our child will have my love for medicine or yours for dance. We have to wait for the answers to all those questions, but the ultrasound can tell us one thing about our baby—whether it's a boy or a girl."

His confession moved me to the point where there was only one possible answer. "Call Dr. Frazier back in, and let's find out the sex of our baby."

Declan dropped one last kiss on my lips and walked over to the door. As soon as he cracked it open, Dr. Frazier peeked her head in. "What's the verdict?"

"We'd like to know, please."

She beamed a smile my way at my response. "I'm not surprised. Dr. McGowan can be fairly persuasive when he wants to be." I darted a wary gaze between the two of them, wondering what she meant by that, and relaxed when she continued. "He's done an excellent job talking donors out of money for the new pediatrics wing. It's just too bad it won't be done before your little girl is born since the wing will also be the home to new labor and delivery rooms."

"Little girl?" I gasped.

"Hot damn!" Declan whooped, scooping me off the exam table and twirling me around. "A baby girl who's going to be just as beautiful as her mommy."

"Maybe she'll look like her daddy instead," I suggested shyly, gazing up at him when he set me on my feet.

Declan wasn't the least bit self-conscious about Dr. Frazier watching us in such a personal moment. He cradled my face in his palms and captured my lips, kissing me tenderly. It might not have been the right time or place, considering Declan worked there, but it was exactly what I needed to feel closer to him. Lost in the kiss, neither of us heard the door click shut as we physically expressed all the emotions the ultrasound had evoked inside.

His thumbs swept across my cheeks when he lifted his head and stared down at me. Then he dropped to his knees and whispered against my belly, "Hello in there, baby girl McGowan. This is your daddy. I love you very much and can't wait to meet you, my little peanut."

Cue the tears—again. Although this time it was more than just stupid hormones. I was thrilled my baby girl had her daddy's unconditional love. I just wished I did, too.

"Do you have to go into the studio today?" Declan murmured from the bed.

I stepped out of the walk-in closet, dressed for a day full of dance classes, and let my eyes linger on his naked chest. The sheet hung low on his hips, his eyes were sleepy, and his dark hair was tousled after a night spent making love to celebrate the news about our baby girl. We'd popped into his office after the ultrasound so he could get some work done, but we hadn't stayed long. After a quick, early dinner, we'd spent the rest of the night in bed. Forget champagne and cake, sex with Declan was the best way to celebrate.

This morning was a return to the real world though, and I had to leave the private bubble we'd created around ourselves. I would have loved to be able to hide in it, particularly that day, but it just wasn't possible. "I'm meeting with Serena today to talk about the pregnancy."

His eyes narrowed and he tilted his head to the side. "She doesn't know yet?"

"It's only been three days since I found out," I answered defensively. "Since you were able to get me an ultrasound appointment with Dr. Frazier for the same day as my originally scheduled one, I figured it wouldn't hurt to wait until afterwards to let her know."

He rolled out of the bed and stalked towards me, laying his hand gently on my belly when he got close. "You haven't been pushing yourself too hard, have you? I know how important dance is to you, but you're dancing for two now."

"Dancing for two," I repeated dreamily. The baby kicked at his hand, almost as though she knew we were talking about her. "I think that's a sign that she likes the idea of dancing with her mommy as much as I do."

"Maybe, but I think she just loves the sound of her daddy's voice," he teased.

"Then she must take after her mommy because I do too."

"If you play hooky with me today, I'll whisper sweet nothings in your ear for as long as you like," he offered hopefully.

"Oh, please. We both know you aren't really going to take the whole day off," I answered, wagging my finger at him. "In fact, I'll probably beat you home. Depending on how my meeting with Serena goes, I may be home super early. I'm not sure how she's going to take the news of my pregnancy since I'm already four months along. It's been years since one of the principal ballerinas has been pregnant, and she'd been happily married and trying for a baby for more than a year. This time around, it's going to come as a shock to everyone. If they aren't willing to let me continue with classes throughout the pregnancy, then earning my principle spot back would be incredibly difficult."

"I know how important your career is to you. I think I proved that with how I handled your four-month absence." I shook my head in confusion, but he didn't notice since he was staring down at his hands on my stomach. "You have my support, one-hundred percent, but I want your promise that you'll be careful and won't overdo it out of fear for what will happen after the baby is here. I don't know what I'd do if anything happened to either of my girls."

"You have it," I vowed, linking my fingers through his and holding them against me.

We stood together like that for longer than I'd realized. When we finally broke apart, I had to make a mad dash across town to the studio and was almost late to my meeting with Serena. The company's ballet mistress adored me, but tardiness was one of her biggest pet peeves. It was a fact I was reminded of when I barely made it into her office with one minute to spare and she pointedly looked at the clock on the wall.

"I trust the reason for this meeting is urgent since you almost made me wait for you?"

"I'm four months pregnant," I blurted out, skipping the entire speech I'd practiced in my head for the last couple days.

"Well," she murmured, dropping into her chair with her eyebrows raised as her gaze swept my body. "That would explain the weight gain."

"It's five pounds," I grumbled. "And it was only four the last time you saw me."

"There will be many more pounds to follow, I'm sure. Four months along, you said?"

"Yes, I just found out this week, and had an ultrasound yesterday. It's a girl, and a perfectly healthy pregnancy." I shoved some papers at her that the doctor had given me upon my request. "I've already spoken with my doctor about this, and she's supportive of me continuing with my workout as long as I'm careful and listen to my body's signals."

"You can dance," she conceded after reviewing the information from Dr. Frazier, and I heaved a big sigh of relief. "In classes only, where I can ensure you're being cautious as your body changes throughout the pregnancy. I'll speak with Hayes about your unavailability for casting."

"I don't want to do anything to put my baby at risk," I assured her, feeling relieved that she was going to tackle the conversation with our artistic director for me. "My doctor even said it will help me maintain my body strength, which might alleviate some of pregnancy's negative side effects. Plus, the baby's father"—she sent a pointed look at the ring on my finger, and I corrected myself—"my fiancé is a pediatric surgeon. I've recently moved in with him, and he's going to want to keep a close eye on my health, too, so it's not like I'm going to be able to get away with much, even if I wanted to. Which I don't."

"Yes," she agreed. "We will work to keep your core strong to help you avoid back pain. This we can do, but no performing. No lifts. No grand jetés."

"Whatever you think is best," I agreed.

"Remember, Juliette. You have many years to dance, even though they might not all be on the stage, but you only have so many to become a mother." She looked sad for a moment, and I couldn't help but wonder if she regretted never marrying and having children of her own. The dance world was different when she was a prima ballerina. I was deeply grateful for the changes over the years, which allowed me to live my dream and be a mother too.

Chapter 8

Declan

From just outside the door, I watched Juliette's graceful body float around the empty dance studio. The walls of mirrors magnified her elegance and her ballet slippers gliding along the polished, wooden floors.

Her honey brown hair was twisted into a bun, baring her slender neck. Her slim body was poured into a black leotard, nude tights, and well-loved, pink toe shoes. The lines of her body were only interrupted by the growing roundness of her six-month pregnant belly. She was fucking gorgeous and I was transfixed, unable to look away for fear I would miss one single movement. She was strong and postured, and yet, she moved like liquid, flowing and free.

I would never tire of watching my beautiful ballerina. Every dance step reminded me of the way I loved her, it looked effortless, but I knew it was strong and full of emotion. The last two months had been amazing, living with her, planning our wedding, watching our baby grow. The only downside was that my schedule at the hospital had been packed and I'd missed her like crazy. But, we were about to have a whole week off together while we finalized wedding details. Finally, it couldn't come a moment too soon.

After several more minutes, she came to a stop and carefully walked over to one of the walls, bending down (giving me a spectacular view of her mouthwatering ass) and picking up a tattered notebook. She scribbled something in it, then looked out at the room, her eyes sweeping around as though she was watching something play out in front of her. Her head dipped once more and she wrote furiously as she walked over to a table and set it down. Then a bright smile grew on her sweet lips and it took my breath away.

My heart was racing and my cock was hard and aching. I glanced around, confirming the empty halls. It was after ten and the place was pretty much deserted since the season hadn't yet begun. I stepped inside the room and closed the door behind me with a soft click. Juliette had made her way to the sound system and was searching through her iPhone intently. Between her focus and the music, she didn't hear my entry. One wall of the studio was windows, looking out into the hallways of the building. But, there was a button by the light switch that lowered shades for privacy and I pushed it before striding over to her.

The movement finally caught her attention and she spun around in surprise, losing her balance and tipping right into my arms. *Perfect.* I grinned at her for a moment before claiming her mouth in a deep kiss. The flavor of her kisses were as addictive as the taste of her pussy.

That thought spurred my body into action and I palmed both butt cheeks, lifting her until her legs wrapped around my waist. I could feel the heat of her sex burning through the thin layer of my scrubs and her leotard. *Leotard. Fuck.* That thing was like a fucking chastity belt. Luckily, I happened to know Juliette had plenty of others, so I felt zero remorse when I slid my hand between us and ripped a hole through the stretchy fabric, as well as her tights.

She gasped and reared back, glaring at me. "Declan!" Her eyes darted around nervously.

"Relax, baby," I purred. "Even if this place wasn't deserted, no one can see us, or hear us over the music."

"But, my clothes—"

"Yeah," I grumbled. "We're going to need to do something about those. I need easy access."

She sputtered as I pivoted and walked over to the wall sporting the ballet barre. I set her down right in front of it and turned her to face the mirror. Her skin was flushed and she looked like she'd been thoroughly kissed. I placed hot, wet, open-mouthed kisses along her neck and nuzzled the sensitive spot behind her ear. She shuddered and moaned, amplifying my need.

"Hold onto the barre, baby," I whispered, then waited for her to grip it tight. Giving a little squeeze of her hips, I encouraged her to go up onto the toes of her slippers. It put her at just the right height for my cock to nestle into the crack of her ass. Her cheeks were round and firm, pressing against me in the most delicious form of torture. I needed her.

Slipping a hand under one leg, I lifted it and straightened it out so it rested on the barre, opening her up. I loved how flexible she was, it made our sextivities a lot more adventurous.

Keeping one hand on her hip to help steady her, I brought the other around to her front and dipped it into the wide, round neckline of her body suit to play with one of her hard nipples. I twisted and plucked it, enjoying her moans and the way her firm little ass pressed even harder against my dick. Watching her face in the mirror, her violet eyes cloudy with passion, had me on the verge of coming.

After showing both tits equal attention, my hand traveled down, caressing her stomach, then onto the tear in her outfit. I dragged my index finger through her pussy lips and lifted it to show her the glistening digit.

"You're so wet, Jules. Fucking soaked. I love how much I turn you on." I sucked my finger clean and groaned, "You taste so damn good, baby."

Lust roared through my body and I couldn't wait any longer. I practically tore my scrubs trying to extricate my cock, then used my free hand to line him up and thrust hard and deep into her drenched pussy.

"Keep holding the barre, Juliette, and lock your knee, so it doesn't buckle." With both hands on her hips, I drove into her over and over, staring at the picture we made in the floor to ceiling reflective glass.

Juliette cried out with each plunge inside her and her head dropped back, her eyes closed. "Open your eyes, baby," I demanded softly. "I want you to see what we look like, how perfect we are together. Let me see your beautiful eyes while I fuck you from behind. I want to see you come in this position."

She dragged her lids up and met my gaze, fire swirling in their depths. "I want," she panted, "to see you too."

"You will, baby," I grunted. "But first, I'm going to make you come so fucking hard. Starting tonight, I get you all to myself for a week and I'm going to make sure you feel me every time you move when the week is over."

My words sent her skyrocketing up, reaching for her orgasm, and her eyes began to close. I released one hip and slapped her ass before I growled, "Eyes!"

They flung open and I bent my knees for a deeper angle, reaching around to pinch her clit. She screamed my name as she shattered and her walls squeezed my cock in a death grip, milking my orgasm along with hers. I shuddered violently, dizzy with the force of it. But, I held tight to her, keeping her steady and safe.

When both our bodies were nearer to calm, I righted our clothes, well as best I could for her, and swept her up into my arms. I strode over and set her on the table while I hefted her small duffle bag up off the ground and set it next to her.

Unzipping it, I pulled out sweat pants and a hoodie, then helped her into them while she stared dreamily at me with a loopy smile. I shook my head and chuckled. "You're fucking adorable, you know that?"

She grinned, shut off the sound system, and hopped off the table to fling her arms around my neck and kiss me. I was tempted to go for round two, but I wanted to get my girls home. I had a sneaking suspicion Juliette had forgotten to eat. She was pretty good about it, but sometimes she got caught up in her work and didn't remember food.

"Let's get home, baby. Then you can ravish me all you want." The sweet sound of her laughter echoed in the room and warmed every inch of me. I unwound her arms and drew one around my waist as I draped mine over her shoulders. I grabbed the duffle and we headed for the door. After unlocking it, we stepped into the hall and started for the exit.

The room next door was open and a woman with black hair and striking green eyes was just shutting off the light and closing the door. She looked us over, her darkly painted lips twisting as though she'd been sucking on lemons.

Both women paused and I glanced down at Juliette. Her spine was ram-rod straight, and her chin raised stubbornly, but she was blushing fire-engine red and I had to stifle a laugh at the sight.

"Juliette," the woman greeted stiffly.

"Hello, Irina," Juliette responded in kind. "Have a pleasant evening." Then she gripped my waist tighter and urged me forward. We walked out into the night, relatively quiet for New York, but then Lincoln Center wasn't a place for nightlife in the off season. I cuddled Juliette close as we took the red line to our apartment in Chelsea. Then I spent the night working on my goal to brand her body and make sure there was no question who she belonged to.

"Fucking hell," I breathed, completely stunned. Much to my delight, Juliette wasn't very traditional and had allowed me to accompany her to help pick out a wedding dress.

She'd tried on four dresses and as she walked out of the dressing room in the fifth, I was blown away. She was so beautiful it almost hurt. Well, actually, it did hurt because my groin was stiff and ready for me to rip the dress right off of her.

It was strapless, the top made of a rich, black velvet, made up of diagonal folds all the way around. It hugged her breasts and with the dipped neckline, it gave her sexy as fuck cleavage. A wide, satiny black sash settled just above her bump with a matching flower attached at the right side. My eyes continued downward, following an airy, flowing, white fabric all the way to the floor. Doing a second perusal back up, I went all the way to her head where she'd put on a headband that mirrored the sash, with white netting covering a portion of her face.

"Do you like it?" she asked hesitantly. "I know it's not the traditional all white, but—I—"

I stood and swiftly approached her, pulling her into my arms and kissed her senseless. "It's perfect," I whispered when I pulled away. "Now go change before I accidentally rip it while I fuck you in the dressing room."

Her skin turned a charming shade of pink but her eyes flared with desire. It took all of my strength to turn her around and urge her back into the dressing room with a light smack on her ass.

I sat down to wait, more than ready to get my girl home and in bed. Although, we had one more stop to make, the stop I'd earned in the bargain when she convinced me to participate in all of the wedding prep over the week we had off together. Juliette was a no-nonsense kind of woman and she'd been quick and decisive with all of the decisions she'd had to make. In the end, I really hadn't minded being dragged along to all of the appointments. But, I was still going to make her hold up her end of the deal.

She emerged from the changing room, back in her street clothes and spoke with the clerk for a few minutes. The other woman took the dress and went through a door at the back of the store. With my hand on her lower back, I guided Juliette to the front and pulled out my wallet to pay for the garment.

"No, Declan," she protested. "I've let you pay for everything else." Only after I'd used my powers of persuasion to convince her to stop arguing with me about it. "But, if my parents were alive, they would be paying for my dress. It's the bride's responsibility!"

I tugged her into the circle of my arms and kissed the tip of her nose. "Baby, I would have convinced them to let me pay for everything, so you might as well stop fighting it. Besides, how many times do I have to explain how this works? We're getting married. What's mine is yours and"—I surreptitiously slid a hand between us and cupped her pussy, grinning when she gasped—"what's yours is mine."

"Declan!" she hissed, looking around frantically. I kissed her nose again and took advantage of her distracted state to whip out my credit card and pay for the dress.

She grumbled all the way to our next stop, causing the cab driver to throw me looks of pity, to which I responded with a wide, satisfied smile. He then looked at me like I'd lost my mind. I could only assume the man had never had a woman like Juliette, or he would have understood. His look of envy when we pulled up to the exclusive lingerie boutique was icing on the cake. Until he stared at Juliette's ass as she climbed out of the car. I growled in warning and lowered his tip to almost non-existent. *Bastard.*

We left the store with two large, red shopping bags and hailed another cab. I glared at the driver from the moment he pulled up and he wisely averted his eyes. Juliette noticed this time and rolled her eyes before sliding across the bench seat. But her cheeks were a little pink and a smile was playing around the corners of her lips.

Despite her vocal denials to the contrary, she loved how possessive I was of her. I hauled her across the seat and snuggled her into my side. I couldn't wait to get home and dig through the bags of new treasures.

But, when we finally got home, Juliette burst my bubble by informing me that the bags were for the honeymoon and proceeded to store them away in the closet while I stood back, mouth hanging open in shock.

Chapter 9

Juliette

Whoever it was who said 'time flies when you're having fun' sure knew what they were talking about. The week I spent with Declan getting everything ready for the wedding was one of the best of my life. Unfortunately, it felt like it flew by in the blink of an eye. If Declan hadn't been up and out the door at the butt crack of dawn, I wasn't sure I'd have been able to drag mine out of bed to leave for the studio on time. I'd quickly become addicted to lazy mornings spent in bed with him.

Although, I'm not sure lazy was quite the right word for it. Declan had decided the best exercise routine during my time off was one which included a whole lot of horizontal action—with him as my very own personal trainer. I wasn't about to argue, not when it meant I was able to stay in shape while enjoying tons of orgasms. It was the best kind of win-win situation for me, but it had come to an end and I was ready to make the most of the next few months in the studio before the baby came.

Serena had suggested I try my hand at choreography since my practice hours were limited by my pregnancy. I'd been hesitant at first, but I'd quickly fallen in love with my new creative outlet. There was one particular piece I was excited to show her and our artistic director today. I'd had a breakthrough in my composition that last night at the studio. After running through it in my head over and over again during my time away, I was certain it was exactly the way I wanted it.

The first thing I did when I arrived was to find Serena. "Hey," I greeted her when I peeked my head into her office.

"Welcome back." Her eyes drifted down to my belly and a big grin split her face. "You look amazing. Your time off must have been exactly what you needed."

"It was perfect," I agreed. "So much so that I think the piece I've been working on the last couple months is done."

"You have fantastic timing!" She jumped up from her seat and hurried towards me, grabbing my hand and leading me down the hall to the largest studio. "Hayes is running through a couple new pieces today, so you can show both of us at the same time. He has a nice selection of dancers in there for you to pick from, and it should only take them a few run-throughs before they'll be ready to show us what you've got."

Butterflies took flight in my stomach at the thought of watching my fellow dancers performing the first piece I'd choreographed on my own in front of our artistic director, Leonard Hayes. I was already nervous about Serena's feedback, but I knew she wouldn't be too harsh. She would be constructive rather than harsh, even if she hated it. Plus, she'd liked the parts I'd already shown her. Hayes was a whole different story since he could be a bit of a jerk about other people's choreography at times.

Apparently, this wasn't one of those days since he was raptly watching several of the corps members perform. The piece was beautiful, undeniably so . . . it was also hauntingly familiar. It was the same exact one I'd been working to perfect during my last night at the studio a week ago! I hadn't thought anyone had seen me. I hadn't even known any other dancers were in the building at the time, not until we'd bumped into Irina in the hallway on our way out.

Irina! I searched the room for that black-haired bitch, and there she was—standing in the corner of the room next to Hayes with a smug smirk on her face. *Why that little...* It was terribly difficult to resist marching my pregnant self over there and punching her right in the face. She'd stolen my choreography! Down to every little step, without even bothering to change a single move. The gall of that woman never ceased to amaze me.

"She's got balls. Giant, brass ones. I'll give her that but not much else," I muttered.

"Oh, I've got something to give her all right," Serena snarled from behind me. "A swift kick on her behind on her way out the door."

My dance mistress marched over to where Irina stood and flashed her a smile which looked obviously fake to me.

"Such magnificent choreography," she cooed.

Irina's face lit up with pride. "Thank you, Mistress."

"And so different from your usual style."

"You've always encouraged us to push our own boundaries," Irina explained.

"It really is a major accomplishment," Serena offered, and Irina practically preened with excitement at the compliment—only to find herself crashing back to reality when Serena continued. "For the dancer who actually choreographed the piece, who we both know was most definitely not you."

You could have heard a pin drop in the silence following her announcement before Irina started to sputter. "What? Why would you even suggest such a thing? Of course I did!"

Serena switched her focus to Hayes. "The girl is lying."

"I am not!" Irina screeched.

"I'm not sure how you thought you'd get away with stealing Juliette's work, but I know beyond a shadow of a doubt that this is her piece."

"Why? Did your little teacher's pet tell you it's hers in a desperate attempt to remain relevant since she can't dance anymore?" Irina hissed.

"No, Irina. Because I've seen part of this dance as she's worked on it over the last two months. She's come to me for advice and asked for my feedback, just like I'd expect any dancer new to choreography to do. Can you say the same? Is there anyone who's seen you work on this piece?"

"Yes, just this past week—"

Serena didn't let her finish. "Do you think I'm dumb? That I don't know a dance I've already seen? That it's purely coincidence you worked on this piece during the one week when Juliette was absent?"

"Is this true, Irina?" Hayes asked.

"I—I—I don't—" she stammered.

"Leave," he ordered, pointing one long finger towards the door.

"And take your things with you because we have no room for a dancer capable of such duplicity in our company," Serena added.

"My notebook," I interjected, realizing that's why it hadn't been in the lost and found when I'd called. "Please make sure she doesn't pack it along with her stuff. I'd like to get it back."

Irina stormed towards the door, and I barely managed to get out of her path before she passed me.

"Fifteen-minute break, everyone," Hayes called out, drawing my attention away from the door. "Juliette, please schedule an appointment with me for this week to discuss possibly using your piece in an upcoming show."

The dancers filed out of the room, whispering about the drama amongst themselves.

"Wow," Lisa murmured as she sidled up next to me, apparently headed in the same direction. "I don't know whether to say congratulations or I'm sorry for all the drama. Are you okay? I mean, I know we haven't really gotten the chance to get to know each other very well, but you are pregnant with my friend's husband's best friend's baby. That sounded way less weird in my head than it did out loud."

A giggle bubbled up my throat, breaking off when I let out a startled yelp at the sound of another voice behind us.

"No wonder my ears were ringing," Nancy joked. "I thought I was going to surprise my friend and see if she could maybe do lunch today, but lunch for three sounds even better."

"Oh, I wouldn't want to intrude," I tried to decline.

"You could never be an intrusion," Nancy assured me. "Not when Kevin and I are thrilled to see Declan head over heels in love with you and so excited for the baby."

"Head over heels in love?"

"Yeah," she sighed, with a dreamy look in her eyes. "Kevin and I were talking about it the other day while we were shopping for your wedding gift. He told me the first time he saw the two of you together, he finally understood why Declan had been such an antisocial grouch for so long. Kevin isn't exactly the most insightful person ever—I mean, well, he is a guy after all—but even he said it was nice to see his best friend finally meet his perfect match."

"I'm such an idiot," I murmured, my head swirling with all the memories of my time with Declan. His gentleness and protectiveness. How possessive he was of me when we were around other men. The time he'd mentioned waiting four months for me while I'd been gone on my international tour. The look in his eyes when we made love. The proud way he'd slid his grandmother's ring onto my finger when he'd proposed. It was all because he loved me.

"Lisa, can you do me a huge favor and make sure Serena gets my notebook from Irina? And tell her I'm sorry but I had to leave unexpectedly?" I asked. She nodded, and I pulled Nancy to me for a quick hug. "I'd love to do lunch with you, just not today."

I barely took the time to grab my purse before I raced out of the building and hopped into the first cab I found. A quick text to Declan confirmed he was in his office, so I headed straight there as soon as the cab dropped me off at the hospital entrance. I didn't bother knocking, just stormed in and threw myself into Declan's lap when I found him in his chair behind his desk.

"Jules, baby, is everything okay?"

"More than okay," I assured him, peppering his face with kisses. "Amazing. Astounding. Wonderful. I can't even come up with a word good enough to explain how okay everything is."

"Good morning at the dance studio?"

"You love me," I breathed out.

"Of course I do." He looked at me curiously, one eyebrow raised and his head tilted to the side.

"And I love you."

"Damn straight you do."

"I love you," I repeated, enjoying how the phrase rolled off my tongue. "So very much, but I'd love you even more if you could say those three little words back to me."

His eyes widened with surprise. "I've never actually said it, have I?" His arms tightened around me. "Fuck, how is that possible when I love you so damn much? From the moment I saw you on stage that first night, I've known you were meant to be mine, Juliette. I'm the luckiest bastard alive because here you are, expecting my baby and with my ring on your finger. I can't wait for our wedding day, for you to become my wife. It's all I've wanted from the beginning, as crazy as it sounds."

"Oh, Declan," I sighed, tears streaming down my face.

"I love you, Juliette Moureaux soon-to-be-McGowan."

His speech was beautiful, but he'd gotten one thing wrong—I was the lucky one.

Epilogue

Declan

I jumped to my feet and clapped my hands so hard they started to sting and turn red. I didn't care, I barely felt it any more than I felt the smile practically breaking my face. A beautiful ballerina glided to the front of the stage and curtsied, holding tight to her pink, fluffy tutu. She grinned brightly, showing off her dimples and sparkling violet eyes. Then she turned to step back into the line of other dancers, but not before waving her chubby little hand at me first.

She was so damn adorable, just like her mother. On the heels of that thought, I was distracted by my gorgeous wife as she stepped onto the stage to deafening applause. I laughed when Cassie darted out of line and ran over to throw her four-year-old arms around Juliette's legs.

Juliette bent down and whispered something in her ear and Cassie giggled before scampering back into place. The crowd died down and the director of the dance school stepped out onto the stage with a microphone.

"We'd like to thank Juliette McGowan for taking the time out of her busy schedule to choreograph a piece for our recital. It was truly an honor to work with such a renowned choreographer and we are grateful New York City Ballet let us steal a bit of her time." She wrapped up the performance with a few other remarks and then dismissed the dancers to find their families.

"Dadadadada! Gah!" I turned my attention to the little boy squirming in Nancy's arms. My son reached for me and I lifted him high, nuzzling his round little tummy. Warmth filled my chest at the sound of Henry's delighted little squeals and the twinkle in his warm brown eyes. Nancy patted his rump and then leaned up on tip toes to kiss my cheek.

"We've got to collect our little monsters and get them home to bed. I'll say goodbye to the girls on the way out, but we'll see you on Thursday, right?"

"Great. My parents will be here on Saturday to pick the kids up from your house. Thanks again for watching them until they could get here."

"Are you kidding? Our kids ignore us when yours are over for a visit. It's like a vacation," Kevin joked.

I snuggled Henry to my chest and followed them out of the auditorium. They took off to find their kids, while Henry and I hung out, waiting for our girls. After a handful of minutes, a bundle of puffy, sparkly pink came barreling into the lobby and over to me.

"Daddy!" she screamed happily as she ran. I shifted my son to one arm and bent down to scoop Cassie up into the other. "Did you see me?"

I smacked a kiss on her cheek before answering, "I sure did, twinkle toes. How could I miss the prettiest ballerina on the stage?" I winked at her and she giggled.

I looked just beyond her and watched Juliette approach. Damn, she was amazing. Her eyes were soft as she looked at the treasures I held in my arms. When she reached us, she wrapped her arms around us and squeezed.

"She did great, didn't she?" Juliette murmured proudly.

"Just like her mommy," I agreed, then kissed her lips softly. "Let's go home."

"I miss my babies," Juliette mumbled tearfully, and I hugged her close into my side. She'd been weepy on and off since we dropped the kids off at Nancy and Kevin's last night. We'd said our goodbyes then because we had an early flight to Hawaii for our anniversary. In fact, she'd been in a state over leaving them on and off for over a week. I was familiar with these mood swings, plus she'd been feeling sick, and I wondered when she would catch on to the fact that she was pregnant again.

Her head rested on my chest and I dropped a kiss on her crown. "They are going to have so much fun, Jules. They won't even know we're gone."

She sniffed and nodded. Clearly, she needed a distraction. With one long finger, I lifted her chin and covered her mouth with mine, lazily sweeping my tongue into her mouth and groaning at her delicious taste. A little moan escaped her mouth and I felt a shiver run through her. Before things could get out of hand, I pulled back and simply gazed at her. She was fucking gorgeous with her flushed skin and lust glazed, violet eyes.

"Hmmm, I'm not sure I'll be able to get my fill of your sexy ass in ten days, baby," I growled in her ear. I was mentally talking myself out of dragging her into the bathroom and joining the mile-high club.

She chuckled and patted the obvious bulge in my slacks. "Patience, Dec." I glared at her but couldn't help falling victim to her charms when she smiled and lightly brushed her lips over mine.

"Ahem." We looked up to see a first class flight attendant waiting for our attention, a small smile playing around the corners of her mouth. "Newlyweds?" she asked slyly.

Juliette giggled and I cuddled her closer. "Anniversary," I answered.

"Ah, congratulations! Would you like some champagne?"

Juliette opened her mouth but I cut her off. "No, thank you. I'll have water and my wife will have apple juice." Then thinking about Juliette's last two pregnancies, I added, "With a little Sprite." The woman was clearly surprised, but she simply nodded and moved onto the next row.

Juliette frowned at me. "I wanted so—" She broke off when the plane hit an air pocket and her face practically turned green. She threw off her seat belt and tore down the aisle to the bathroom. I followed quickly behind, ready to take care of my woman. She was all too grateful for the Sprite later on and the rest of the flight was relatively uneventful.

Eleven hours later, we were finally pulling up to our hotel. I unloaded our bags from the rental car and set them inside the bungalow, then returned to carry my wife over the threshold. She laughed but allowed me the silly gesture, her cheeks turning pink with that blush I still loved to see.

I kicked the door shut and flipped the lock, then walked over and set her down. She traipsed over to the bathroom to freshen up while I unpacked a few things. When she stepped back into the room, I pressed a button on my phone and grabbed her hand, tugging her into my arms. "Dance with me, baby," I crooned and began to sway to the beat.

We slowly moved around the room until I danced her over to the bed and laid her down. I was out of patience. Making quick work of our clothes, I sighed in relief when our naked bodies were pressed together.

"In a hurry there, Dec?" she asked on a laugh.

"Baby," I sighed. "Henry has been sick and you and I have been working extra hours to get everything done so we could take off. We haven't had more than a quick fuck in almost three weeks. I can't help it if I'm desperate to feel you against me, I want to savor it. In fact," I mused, "I think I'll keep you naked for the next ten days."

Juliette chuckled and wrapped her arms around me tightly. "Deal," she whispered in my ear.

"I hope you don't think I'm joking, Mrs. McGowan," I replied archly. I *so* wasn't.

"Declan, shut up and make love to me."

I grinned salaciously. "But, you like it when I talk." I sucked the lobe of her ear into my mouth and bit it gently. Then whispered, "It drives you wild when I say filthy things while I fuck the hell out of you."

She moaned and squirmed restlessly.

I started to kiss my way down her body. "Let's see how many times I can remind this sweet pussy who owns it over the next ten days."

Much . . . much later, I gathered Juliette up so her back was pressed up against my front. I lay a hand over her belly and grinned, nuzzling my nose in her soft hair.

She sighed. "You knocked me up again, didn't you?"

I laughed and hugged her closer. "You bet your ass I did. My boys know how to get the job done."

She poked me in the ribs with her elbow but the side of her face scrunched, letting me know she was smiling. Her hand joined mine over her belly and she sighed again.

I'd never admit it to Nancy, but I would be forever grateful I let her guilt me into attending the ballet all those years ago. I had no idea what I'd done to deserve such a fucking perfect life and I knew it would only get better from there.

Books By This Author

About the Author

Hello! My name is Fiona Davenport and I'm a smutoholic. I've been reading raunchy romance novels since... well, forever and a day ago it seems. And now I get to write sexy stories and share them with others who are like me and enjoy their books on the steamier side. Fiona Davenport is my super-secret alias, which is kind of awesome since I've always wanted one.

You can connect with me online on Facebook or Twitter.

Made in the USA
Lexington, KY
23 March 2018